In Lucia's Neighborhood

Pat Shewchuk • Marek Colek

Kids Can Press

To those who planted flowers, swept sidewalks, sat on porches, played in the festivals and made the neighborhood a nice place to live.

Kids Can Press acknowledges the financial support of the Government of Ontario, through the Ontario Media Development Corporation's Ontario Book Initiative; the Ontario Arts Council; the Canada Council for the Arts; and the Government of Canada, through the CBF, for our publishing activity.

Published in Canada by
Kids Can Press Ltd.
25 Dockside Drive
Toronto, ON M5A 0B5

Published in the U.S. by
Kids Can Press Ltd.
2250 Military Road
Tonawanda, NY 14150

www.kidscanpress.com

The artwork in this book was rendered digitally.
The text is set in Myriad Pro.

Edited by Yvette Ghione
Designed by Julia Naimska

This book is smyth sewn casebound.
Manufactured in Shenzhen, China,
in 9/2012 through Asia Pacific Offset.

CM 13 0 9 8 7 6 5 4 3 2 1

FSC
www.fsc.org
MIX
Paper from responsible sources
FSC® C012521

Library and Archives Canada Cataloguing in Publication

Shewchuk, Pat
   In Lucia's neighborhood / written and illustrated by Pat Shewchuk and Marek Colek.

For ages 3–7
ISBN 978-1-55453-420-3

I. Colek, Marek II. Title.

PS8637.H4897I6 2012   jC813'.6   C2011-905064-

Kids Can Press is a **corus**™ Entertainment company

"The ballet of the good city sidewalk never repeats itself from place to place, and in any one place is always replete with new improvisations."

Jane Jacobs
The Death and Life of Great American Cities, 1961

My name is Lucia.

My grandmother has been telling me about Jane Jacobs. She was a lady who talked about neighborhoods.

She talked about the people in them, the things they do and what makes a neighborhood nice.

She talked about neighborhoods like mine.

This story is about my neighborhood.

About the people I see. The work they do.
The houses they live in.

About the things that happen here every day.

My neighborhood is pretty busy in the morning.

People are going to work, going to school
or going to the park!

The park is great.

All kinds of people go there —
big people,
medium people
and little people.

I really like the Tai Chi people.

I see them practicing every morning.

There are also joggers and dog walkers.

All the dog walkers let their dogs run free in the off-leash area.

The dogs really like it.

Soon the shops start to open.
The workers have lots of work to do.

Coffee
and a
Muffin
$2.50

The neighbors do, too.
Flowers have to be bought.

Yards must be made beautiful!

Some yards have flowers.
Other yards have sculptures.

Some yards even have tree sculptures!
And some trees are trimmed just like the olive trees in Portugal.

Look! Here comes the letter carrier.
It must be twelve o'clock.

Some kids are coming
home from daycare.

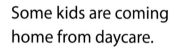

School kids are coming
home for lunch.

Yum! Grandmother
made my favorite soup!

In the afternoon, everyone has somewhere to go and someone to see. There's a lot to talk about.

Every summer there's a parade
for the *Senhor Da Pedra* Festival.

My street is decorated just like in Portugal.
Everybody makes the decorations together.
But my favorite part will come next.

I love to listen to the
band marching down
the street.

I've been daydreaming
about it for weeks!

At the end of the day, people come
home for dinner and things quiet down.

After dinner, everybody's out again.
People sit on their porches. Kids play in their yards.
Grandmas sit in the sun. Teenagers hang out.
Some people head up to College Street.

Some people go out for a late dinner.
Others do a little shopping.

Everybody likes this shop. It has fresh
fruits and vegetables at good prices.

Time to go home!

At night, College Street is still busy.

But my street is pretty quiet.
Just a few people are still out.

When I see Mr. Ferrara going back to work, I know it's time for bed.

And that's the end of my story. The story of an average day in my neighborhood.